Ollie's Halloween

Olivier Dunrea

Houghton Mifflin Books for Children

Houghton Mifflin Harcourt

Boston New York

Houghton Mifflin Books for Children is an imprint of Houghton Mifflin Harcourt
Publishing Company.

www.hmhbooks.com

The text of this book is set in MShannon.
The illustrations are pen and ink and gouache on 140-pound d'Arches coldpress watercolor paper.

Library of Congress Cataloging-in-Publication Data

Dunrea, Olivier.
  Ollie's Halloween / written and illustrated by Olivier Dunrea.
      p. cm.
  Summary: Dressed in their costumes, Ollie and his siblings go out on Halloween night and have
a scary but fun adventure.
  ISBN 978-0-618-53241-4
  [1. Stories in rhyme. 2. Geese—Fiction. 3. Halloween—Fiction.] I. Title.
  PZ8.3.D9266Ol 2010
  [E]—dc22
2009049699

Manufactured in China / LEO 10 9 8 7 6 5 4 3 2
4500288343

For the five wee goblins
in my life—
Johnny, Molly, Gabe,
Peedie, and Fergus

This is Gossie.
She is a wizard.

This is Gertie.
She is a chicken.

This is Peedie.
He is a dragon.

This is BooBoo.
She is a bunny.

This is Ollie.

He is a mummy.

It's Halloween night.
A night to beware.

A night to scare.
Goslings are on the prowl!

Hooting like owls.
Howling like wolves.

Creeping through bogs.
Scaring frogs.

Gossie and Gertie poke
around the pumpkins.

Peedie and BooBoo creep
behind the beehives.

Ollie stalks in the cornfield.

Gossie and Gertie gobble
treats in the haystacks.

Peedie and BooBoo gobble
treats in the cornstalks.

Ollie stares at a ghost in
the open barn door.

"Boo!" shouts Ollie.

It's Halloween night.
A night to beware.

A night to scare.

Hooting! Howling! Haunting!

Goslings bob for apples
in the wooden tub.

In the meadow the scarecrow
shivers in the wind.
Thunder rumbles.

Lightning flashes.
Goslings run back to the barn!

Gossie and Gertie, Peedie
and BooBoo, feast on the
last pile of treats.

Ollie stands
alone in the dark.

It's Halloween night.

A night to share.